Shades of Love

Flairs and Glairs

Publication House

"Shades of Love"

ISBN No: " 978-93-90416-40-0"
1st Edition
Language – English and Hindi

Flairs and Glairs
Publication House
Regd. Under MSME Act.

Disclaimer

This is a work of fiction and solely represent the thoughts of the corresponding authors of the articles. Our editors have tried their best to edit the content of all the authors and check the plagiarism.

All the write-ups in this book are unique and are only published in this book.

In case any plagiarism or error is found, only the author is responsible alone, and not the publisher or the Compilers.

Cover Designing and Book Formatting
Shubham Shah and Ishani Agarwal

Co-Authors

Shubham Shah (Founder Flairs and Glairs)
Ishani Agarwal (Co-Founder Flairs and Glairs)

Sona Agarwal (Compiler)
Rhagavi (Co Compiler)
Surbhi Gupta (Project Head)
1. Shalini.S
2. Malini.S
3. Faheema Banu
4. Saraswetha
5. Sharmila
6. Raihana
7. Kathijathul Kubra
8. Lena Harithaa
9. Gayathri
10. Nikkita Antonette Glasford
11. Sangutharani
12. Jacob Rosario
13. Vishnudevi Saravanan
14. Sofiya Mehake
15. Kowsalya Thangadurai
16. Vaishali Lakshmanan
17. Saicharu
18. Monisha.T
19. Devraj V Pimputkar
20. Suwathiga
21. Jayasankari
22. Saranya
23. Logapreetha
24. Arthy

25. Deebika
26. Vishnu Priya
27. Diksha
28. Ankita Khataniar
29. Hajirabee
30. Sushma Robert
31. Jaya sood
32. Pooja
33. Praveena Ramesh
34. Vibhor Bijoy
35. Rose F.Menezes
36. Valli
37. Arun Albert
38. Adlin
39. Subalakshmi
40. Kumaran Dharmaseelan
41. Venessa Albuquerque

Shubham Shah

(Founder- Flairs and Glairs)

Shubham Shah, an entrepreneur at "Flairs & Glairs" a brand with dynamics in events organizing and cultural educational pan INDIA, is a 26yrs old guy who recently has entered the digital platform of imprinting emotions. He has initiated with

his own open mic platform to help budding poets and aspiring writers under his brand named as "Teekhe Zasbaaat"

He is a commerce graduate from the Bhagalpur City of Bihar.

He states Writing has impersonated him since childhood and he has now been writing for over a decade!

Cooking, on the other hand, is his passion! He also mentions, trying out new things just tickles him!

When asked sir, Why SPICY EMOTIONS?

He smiled and added, "agar jasbaat teekhe na ho toh wo jasbaat kahan" Spices are all that blends! So do his words!

As a chef, he presents to you his dish! Hot and freshly served! Taste it! Feel it! Enjoy it! You can also find his writing in the Book "Teekhe Zasbaaat" and 50+ Co-authored anthologies. With his passion to explore opportunities across Platforms, he is working with keen devotion and We wish him all the very best for his future ventures.

He is Featured in the **International Magazine De-Mode** for his upcoming solo novel.

He is **Approved by Ne8x for its Lit Fest,** and is a **Golden Star Awards 2020 Winner.**

He is an **India Book of Records Holder** for his Anthology **Satrang,** and has the **Grandmaster** title by **Asia Book of Records**, for the same.

He has also been featured in **Prabhat Khabar, Dainik Jagran** and other renowned Newspaper for his achievements. He has also been awarded with **India Star Republic Award 2021.**

He has been a proud co-author to

India Book of Records (Title- Black)

World Book of Records (Title -15 Wonders of Poetries)

India Book of Records (Title - Aaina)
Vajra World Records Holder (Title - Gustakhi Maaf Hai)
High Range of Records Holder (Title - Gustakhi Maaf Hai)

Share your reviews on his

INSTAGRAM
@spicy_emotions
@shubham4shah
Or via email on
shubham2shah@gmail.com

To stay tuned to his work and opportunities follow his business Handles

INSTAGRAM   FACEBOOK   YOUTUBE

@flairsandglairs
@teekhezasbaaat

WEBSITE:
https://flairsandglairs.in/
https://flairsandglairs.com/

Ishani Agarwal

(Co-Founder- Flairs and Glairs)

Ishani Agarwal hails from the City of Joy, Kolkata.
She is the co-founder of her Community "Teekhe Zasbaaat"
and Flairs and Glairs Publication.
Been a Compiler for 45+ Anthologies, she is in the process
for more. Co-authored in 150+ Anthologies. She is a India
Book of Records Holder, a Vajra World Records Holder, a
High Range of Records Holder and a Bravo Record holder.

Approved by Ne8x for its Lit Fest 2020, and Literary Icon 2020. Also a Golden Star Awards Winner 2020.

She has also been awarded with India Star Republic Award 2021.

She has been featured by the National Magazine "Taree Zameen Par" with the title 'unstoppable'.

Also featured in the International Magazine DeMode for her upcoming solo novel, she is proud to write on social issues, and is happy with the love she is receiving.

Connect with her on Instagram: @Ishani_agarwal_quotes / @compilations_so_far

SONA AGARWAL
(COMPILER)

SONA AGARWAL is pursuing her graduation in the field of commerce, residing in Villupuram town within TamilNadu. She loves to enjoy the every moment of the life instead of doing or travelling in single path. She doesn't needed any fame for her works instead of which she needed to enjoy the journey in every possible way till her heart fills up. She writes not to fill the pages with words but with feelings from her heart. The feelings play a major role for every writer. The heart seeks the feelings not the words after all. Her Instagram handle is @ahana__writes

SEPTEMBER 13

I just remember that day,
I have fallen for you,
The corridor I ran with,
Still covered my sight.

You were playing behind,
My eyes searched you tho,
The seats became cushions,
In love with you.

Why the steps are long?
The boards were filled,
In the water of era,
I used to be.

You changed my everything,
Became a part of me,
Why still the day,
Is having a lucky impact?

The cool breeze,
Makes me tie with you,
The love which we made,
Will carry till our last beat.

Shall I whisper one thing?
Don't want to be your first,
But the last thought when you sleep,
Shall I take over it? My love

ARRIVED GIFT

Hey love,
You are my upcoming gift,
The life after a scariest loudness!

The vampire of the hell,
Finally found a good corner,
To settle me up with you!

You are that miracle,
The days for whom I longed for,
Now the meet is not more far!

Grabbing soon our hearts for each,
You are the first soul,
Who craved for me!

And atlast you are the final one,
Who took me away with you,
Forever and ever!

Hold my hands love,
Don't ever skip my heartbeat,
Even for a while and then!

Let we make us for our future,
To be delighted and enlightened,
You are not less than a gift for me!

Love me without any doubt,
Hold me without any intentions,
Just you and me, finally make us.

RHAGAVI
(CO-COMPILER)

RHAGAVI hails from Tamilnadu, she is a girl with million dreams.She discovered her passion in literature few years ago and started scribbling her thoughts out.She hopes to write more and more to support people virtually, she believes her words could make someone smile somewhere and she is trying hard to make everyone believe in the universe. She can be contacted at rhagvisha73@gmail.com. Her IG handle is @secretbehindwords

ISNT'T IT LOVE

Love isn't in the words you speak,
It's in the way you behave,
Love isn't in the secrets you hide,
It's in the truth you seek.

Love isn't in the door of lies,
It's in the home of confessions,
Love isn't in the gifts you wrap,
It's in the efforts you make.

Love isn't in the pleasure,
It's in the pain that you wish to have,
Love isn't in the glow of someone's beauty,
But it's in the heart of someone's loyalty.

Love isn't in the past you had,
It's in the hands you hold for the future,
Love isn't in the anger you hold,
It's you on the whole.

NEVER LET GO OF LOVE

We used to think there's a perfect form of love but we humans aren't perfect how can love be then? Every beautiful things has its imperfections and so love is. If you are searching for someone who is as perfect as you have in dream I just wanna make you remember that they don't exist in this reality. And I wanna make you clear that we make mistakes, misunderstandings but that's how we humans are, what matters is the love you have towards each other in that hard times, that spirit you hold not to give up on each other, that is what really matters. That satisfaction you get when you realize that you have someone who is ready to do anything to make you smile. Yeah ofcourse waiting hurts like hell but that doesn't mean you should have trust issues or you should find someone better, if you do is that love? How can you unlove someone? Then did you ever love them? Waiting is the most painful part in a relationship if you can succeed that what else can be a barrier? Some of you leave the person you love not because you didn't love enough but you did and you had a heartbreak, thank yourself for moving on, you did a great job, just think once if you can love someone who doesn't deserve so much then think about the person who deserves, won't it be a beautiful destiny? So never let yourself to hate love. Let love find you. Your Mr.Right or Mrs.Right may not be as same as you dreamt about but he/she will love you more and take care of you till his/her last breath, remember never give up on life or love. Both love and life is as beautiful as you are.

SURBHI GUPTA
(PROJECT HEAD)

Surbhi Gupta, born and raised in Punjab, is currently a Law Student , B.Com honours graduate and an enthusiastic writer as well. She is also working as Project Head for Flairs And Glairs Publications. Having a Lawyer's mind and a writer's heart, her writings are sui generis, relatable, and inspiring. She has compiled 6 anthologies , co-authored in 40+ and currently working on 3 record aiming projects. Various achievements in academics , Legal events and writing platforms are feathers in her cap. Sight and smell of her own book someday is what she aspires to achieve as a writer. Instagram Handle @surbhi_writes

SHADES OF LOVE

Love, comes in various shades
One can love something and someone,
in many beautiful ways

Parent's love can be called multicolored ,
as they are the reason of all aspects of our Life
From giving to birth to bringing us up
and fulfilling our every dearest desires
they are there for us

Lover has symbols of red roses
and red blush on cheeks
but the most prized possession is
the red hearts beloved exchange
is the purest symbol of love

The blue ink when spills
on the white paper,
and smell of the brown book
makes love with the writer within us

Seasons , ever-changing
but also our constant companions
that we meet each year,
the whites of Winter,
yellow of Summers,
Orange autumns,
and multicolor spring,
makes everlasting love to
person living in..

Nature lovers often
keep their eyes wide open

For greens of the fields
browns of mountains,
blues of oceans,
and the orange pink skies,

Life that we love dwells between
the blue sky and green lands
Life that is meant to be lived
and cherish every moment that we can

Hence, love comes in various shades
in many beautiful ways...

SHALINI

She is Shalini from Villupuram. She is doing her graduation in the field of commerce. Her hobby is drawing. She has love on her parents which make her to shower her words in the poem.

*Instagram Handle: _freshfairy_*

DAD, MY RULER

Walk with me dad,
Hold my little hand,
Show the best for me,
At every place,
Today I seek you,
As I need you till last,
Want to be like you,
Brave and smart,
Love you with my heart,
Always you been there,
For me, with me,
No care more than you
Can be utilized by me,
You gone through darkness
Still made my life bright,
You can't say, your feel for me
But I can know it,
With your eyes & action
Forever be with me dad,
We have long way to go.

EVER REPLACED MOM

Without knowing my face,
My colour, and character,
You always took care,
And loved me a lot,
You can't be replaced,
As others don't have,
Your love for us,
Everyone can be,
Replaced by you,
First ever I was born,
Is in your lap,
I always lived,
Every moment with you,
You're every pain,
Makes me cry,
As you are connected,
To my heart.

MALINI

She is Malini S from Villupuram. She is doing her graduation in the field of commerce. Her hobby is drawing. She has love on her parents which make her to shower her words in the poem.

Instagram Handle: artshine26

MAD LOVE ON YOU

To the world you are my dad,
To me you are the world,
For some you are bad,
To me you are gold,
For some you may zero,
To me you are a real hero,
When I make you sad,
I become mad,
When I make you happy,
You gave me chocky,
You are my light,
When I am in night,
You are my love,
One day you showed me a dove,
You are the beat in my heart,
Which always remembered my thoughts.

HEAL ME MOM

Gonna to say my,
Unsaid feelings mom,
Our love, always I cherish,
Whenever I been hungry,
You possessed with care,
Whenever I been angry,
You possessed your love,
You didn't consider,
What am trying to say,
You always loved me,
With heart shedder,
My sadness,
Healed by your happiness,
My anger,
Calmed by your unconditional love,
Whenever I review my thoughts,
You encouraged me,
Don't mistake me that,
I am not in love with you,
I love you till my last,
Just failed to express it.
You are forever in my thoughts.
Love you mom

FAHEEMA BANU

She is Faheema Banu. She is doing her college. She is studying psychology. She loves writing and she wanted to make it as her career. Her hobby is to read books. She is in love with exploring minds and languages. Her wish is to spread positivity and love, with her words.

Instagram Handle: purple_.scribbles, faheema_002

DARK LOVE

I thank nature for giving you,
Even a little piece of you,
Gives me a lot of peace.
You give me comfort and
Takes away my pain
The lonelier I'm with you,
The more strongly I'll rise up.
Only you know my tears, that
Tear out from my eyes...
Only to you, I've said my sadness
Because you maintain your chillness...
You make me think deep, also
You give me good sleep.
When I stare upon you, your
Pretty winkle glares upon me.
Oh, how beautiful you are!
The silence you have, removes the violence I have.
Though you are not visible,
You have creatures beautifully immiscible.
Staying within you, all I'm
Writing is about you, my love!

FAITH IN HOPE

Though you are treated inferior,
You feel yourself superior
You are not a fool,
Don't desire for a fruit,
Make a wish for a seed.
Though you are feeling ill,
Without the freedom full,
Remember, you can be successful
Never let the hands to hold you...
You hold the hands.
No money and things make you happy
But your smile and time will...
Don't get rid,
Break the circle and explore the world
Though you have a broken heart,
Fix it up with your lovely art
Do what you think
And make you pink...
Share the going trend
With your trusted friend
Don't get afraid, your hope
Can raid the whole sadness.
It's not too late...
Maybe your eyes become more tired and wet...
But your heart and smile always stay fresh.
After losing all your hope,
Being independently, start a journey
Without expectations and
With a New Hope!

SARASWETHA

She is Saraswetha. She is from Villupuram, Tamil Nadu. She is fond of reading books and writing short stories. She writes because of her love for English

Instagram Handle: saras_swetha

HEART'S BREATH

"Can I get a coffee, dear?" I asked my love. She nodded with a smile of assent. Five minutes later, I received my morning coffee with daily newspaper. Seeing her love for me, I remembered our first meeting. I'm Aadhav, an engineering graduate from the University of Amritsar. Now I'm working in a reputed company. That was my first day to college. All the students were in search of their classes including me. Suddenly, a beautiful face struck my mind in that crowd but that lasted only few seconds. Her face attacked my heart with thousands of thunder. After our first day's class, I searched her like a squirrel searching for guava and found her. Her name is Neha. On a Sunday, she went to a coffee shop with her friends which was her usual spot for Sundays. I decided to talk to her with a coincidental style. As she was with her friends, she felt embarrassed to talk with me. But later, in college we met and shared our words. Six months went by. One day I proposed her with full of guts by asking, "Shall we make AN?" She stared at me with confusion. I realized her confusion and cleared up her mind by saying, "I want us to be one, as AN- Aadhav & Neha, I'm in love with you Neha." And I expressed my love for her from my very first sight. She thought for a while and asked me time to decide. She told me to wait till her studies is being completed and she also said that she is elder than me by two years as she joined the college with the lag of two years after her higher education. She told me to wait for three years to know the reason. Her words collapsed me but my love for her made me feel strong and to wait for her. Three years later, I approached her with my heart full of love even more than before three years. She smiled at me with happiness. But suddenly, she became normal and said about her late joining of college, "I had a terrible accident during my

holidays. Due to that I went through a major surgery of heart transplantation and my heart feels weak", said Neha in sad tone. I was shocked by hearing her words, but my love was real for her. So, her age and her problem never made me feel sad. I said, "I love you", in sudden, rather than any other word. She was very happy for my response. We both of us said about our love to our parents. At first, my parents thought about Neha's heart transplantation and regretted, but finally they accepted. I convinced Neha's parents too about their daughter's safety with me. With everyone's heart filled blessings we got married. One year later we were blessed with a baby girl. With our baby in my hand, I said to Neha, "We together made AN." She replied, "Yes" with a smile in her face by recollecting my proposal. We named our little princess as Ananya. Thinking of our golden memories that created our life, I continued my coffee. Now we are leading a very happy life without the fear of Neha's illness. True love lasts till the end of our life and even after the end of our life.

SHARMILA

P.Sharmila, currently doing undergraduate degree in nursing, staying in Pondicherry. She was an eventual writer, loving to write stories at present situation. Interested in writing moral stories inspired from personal life experiences. The story " Louder than words" is about a necessitous boy who cares for love and affection from childhood, fall love on a girl before lockdown who cruelly raped and killed later and how he coped her lost.

Instagram Handle: Sharmila6928sha

LOUDER THAN WORDS

I start my story as everyone start. Once upon a time there lived a boy named Rohit of 18 yrs old; he looks brown with short stature. He is a boy with hope that everything happens for a reason, staying in hostel with a job, less paid. He did not have any aim for the future, lives the life as it goes. No hope on God as he is a child with no love and affection. His parents left him in his childhood in street. A bright morning with warming sun hit his room, his eyes glared through the open window. He woke up suddenly and went to portigo. He went there to see the gorgeous girl with curly hair who carries her dog to a walk. He usually sees her for about a couple of months. She is a girl with very rich background that's the reason why Rohit not approaching her. She used to stay home always basically an introvert and only during weekend she used to go gym for fitness. On Monday, Rohit went to see her friend regarding the job seen in advertisement. His friend was John; he is working in a textile company where he found a job for Rohit. Rohit never bothered about the workload but the salary. How much salary will I get? Asked Rohit. You will be sure able to pay your rent in the first day of a month, said John. Rohit face glowed with joy. The next day all stuffs got ready to the interview, Rohit with a new shirt which was bought months ago but this was the first time he is wearing. The only shirt he had new! Locked the door, walked over the street, waiting for bus in the bus stop. He used to look like strange from being normal. 'May be the new clothes make me strange' Rohit's mind whispered. The girl with gym look crossed him. "Wow! I must be awaiting to see her , thank God! ", he overwhelmed. He didn't think that was the last day he would see her. He cached his bus and attended interview successfully. He came back with full of joy to his room. His only goal is to get job and marry her.

He achieved in getting job so he was happy. Had dinner and went to bed very soon. The next day he thanked his friend going to his home; actually he went to see that girl. But the time doesn't allow him to see. The days went, he sacrifices his appetite, not spent money to buy new clothes or other stuffs. He truly saves her money for his marriage. Even though not knowing where the girl went as he cannot able to see her for last 2 weeks. A little gap between our loved ones also makes us depressed. He lived with her in dream. Walked throughout the street on weekend but he never found his girl. The next day started with a dark cloud, seems to rainy most probably. 'Something happened to me, I feel feverish', feels Rohit. Suddenly a loud noise came next from his room. He, with enlarged ear listened to that noise. The noise was actually news stating "As the novel corona virus pandemic hit our state, our PM announced for a lockdown of 15 days thought-out the country". Rohit doesn't face that situation before. He doesn't know what to do. Asked his neighbor man about the news. He is a nursing officer by profession, hence he said about the pandemic, what is our responsibility, importance of mask and social distancing. Eventhough seems to be understood but actually he is confused still. Stayed at home for about 6 months, lockdown extended, still no lifting of lockdown. The horrible pandemic killed many people and it commences our street lived asymptomatically. He used to listen to neighbor's radio every day. Once he heard a news that a girl named Ruby had been raped by 4 cruel men, the innocent girl tongue made cut, her spine broken very horribly and she was seriously ill in hospital " If girls where good and from literate family this would never happen", neighbor said. Rohit literally apposed his words. There is no meaning for humanity "said himself. He usually doesn't believe God, now he thought not to believe humans too... Rohit were thought full of his girl. Watching through

his window he remembered the past days. Few youngsters were roaming in street; they must be unaware of pandemic I thought. They were not wearing mask, so I as a responsible citizen asked them to wear mask, I didn't expect their answers would be irresponsible, " I am healthy I won't be affected by this small virus!" said the youngster. Then I realized they are aware but ignorant. Few months later, the lockdown lifted but not the pandemic came to an end. I saw the difference between the pre- pandemic and post pandemic life of us; it was a huge difference that is because of the pandemic. I went out searching for my girl, he in sudden saw and poster with her girl. He went near to the poster with tremors. His hands and legs was shaken, sweats lot, his mask got wet his eyes fully open approaching the poster. He was heart- broken, tears filling his eyes, hate the life at that moment, cried aloud in the street. The girl name is Ruby, who is raped by 4 men and killed. He was craving for love. "Why this is happening to me alone, why I should not to be happy? Why all are leaving me, am I born to be cursed? ", he overwhelmed with tears. He quitted his job, stayed alone, watching through window of his room where he used to see that girl every weekend. His feelings are louder than words.

RAIHANA

The Young Author RAIHANA is just 20 who is residing in villupuram and doing her graduation in the field of commerce. She expresses her feelings through some stories which have been actually taken place.

*Instagram Handle: kadaikutty_r.e.o.n_*

WILL YOU BREATHE IN MY HEART?

Love is not about always ending in a happy way, sometimes they live with the memories which they made together and it is irreplaceable for anyone in their lives. This story says about the unfair ending of RISHIQ & SAARA, who were separated by the nature, as the nature only have powers to separate a true one in love. Rishiq a well known Journalist and Businessmen was invited as a Chief Guest at THOMSAN PRESS (INDIA) LIMITED, for their event conducted on 8th of August. After many ongoing speeches, Rishiq was called upon to give an adorable address to the members. After the honorable speech, Rishiq was questioned about how he has achieved this success in his life. Everything in his past has been recollected in front of his heart and mind. He was given voice to be answered and he starts with his childhood, where he has been completed his 6th and were about to enjoy the annual days. On that time, his father has unlatched a Rice Mill and Rishiq even without thinking about the vacations, joins his father and works with him throughout the months. After re-opening of school he goes and by the evening he rejoins the shop as he wanted to be hardworking person in that age too. He has born with sibling, Priya, who is elder than her. The years passed and Rishiq has completed his 9th and worried about after his studies as he wants to appear on board and to look after his father's shop too. By that time he was been introduced to Shifa, who was studying in the tuition where Priya did and was junior to Priya. She came home about gathering the details for her further studies and by sight Rishiq came to know about her. Shifa and Rishiq joined the same school for their higher studies and as days passed by both have been fallen in love too. One day Shifa visits Rishiq's home and he request to go as his mom and Priya will take in a wrong way about their relationship. Shifa feels dejected and leaves, by seeing the droplets under her eyes, Rishiq went behind her. There he pleases for his actions and they talk on the lane. Rishiq's brother Rohit was standing far who has been watching them for a long time and Shifa too often looks at him. Rishiq, who doesn't know about their (Shifa and Rohit) past relationships, came to know by his sister Priya, on that evening. He too acknowledged that Shifa was in relationship with him only for gathering info's about Rohit. Extremely broken Rishiq ended the relationship and focused on his further journey and joined into the college without any interest only for his mother's sayings. For the first week instead of classes, courses were going on and the seniors were the one who were taking it. For Rishiq's department Saara was the senior who have been taking the course. Rishiq's friend Anusham started a friendly go with Saara and Rishiq joined too. After a week, Rishiq blocked the way of Saara and asked the number to contact her and unknowingly by the next day itself they fall for each other and Rishiq has said what and all taken place in his past life and Saara accepted it too. Rishiq was madly in love with her as he obeys each and every instructions of Saara and she too took care of him in a blessing way. Priya's marriage was fixed and by the evening his parents were not available through which Rishiq called Saara to his home with Priya's permission. He snacked her with ice-cream and by the night he dropped her at home too with a sweet long drive on the highway. One day, Rishiq bought a ring which was a couple one. He took Saara for a date and buys her an anklet and presents her instead of the ring. He studies for his final exams and Saara who was the tutor helps in his studying. Suddenly after that he gets news of Saara's accident and run with tears rolling out down there along with the ring too which he bought to present her. After reaching home he was stunned to see the dead body

of Saara and cried out madly and terribly without holding the pain. He takes the ring and wore it by Saara and made her wear another one. He kisses her forehead and keeps a red dot. After burying her body, he, at the funeral cried out terribly and refuses to live his life further for long days. Finally he stood up for her as it was her dream to see Rishiq as a well known business man and a journalist, he by hard working became too. At the burial, he keeps flower and utter that "SAARA, I HAVE BECAME WHAT YOU WISHED FOR", and starts crying. He also says to bless him as it was her dream which he has fulfilled finally, and this time the nature which separated them now helped Saara to bless him with the rain-shower.

KATHIJATHUL KUBRA

She is Kathijathul Kubra, born and bought up in villupuram. She completed her schooling in sacred heart Anglo Indian school, villupuram in 2019 .she is currently pursuing a under graduate degree in commerce field. She is currently working in ifortis corporate company as an intern. She can express anything through her adaptive working style. She has a habit of expressing her thoughts by words. Shades of love is an debt for her as an co-author

WILL I BE YOUR LITTLE PRINCESS????

Love, a most resplendent thing which is "priceless". No one can live without love. When we verbalize about unconditional love I recollect the relationship between father and a daughter. Come on let's look after it. When mother was caring baby in uterus at the month of 6, her Husband was against her. He coerced her to abort baby and fortuitously mother went to hospital with tears to abort her child. The reason for abortion is that, they already have one daughter and son. After mother consulting with medico, everybody was yare to abort baby and at the last moment she called her father and verbalized about this condition. Her father after hearing this gone shattered and then he suddenly reached to hospital to preserve the baby and mother. Her father consulted with medico, then he stopped to abort the child, the mother was ecstatic. At the time mother was teared up while leaving home. When she returns after auricular discerning the news of preserving her child, she returns with the shower of ecstasy in her face, but her husband was exasperated about it and later after consummating ten months, a gorgeous daughter born on 29/11/2001. Everyone was jubilant about the birth and her husband too was ok with it. After spending more time with her daughter, she became minuscule princess for him. He realized the unconditional love for his daughter. The baby's mother was working in a regime school as a pedagogic, so the full care was taken by her father. The father was very fortuitous after the birth of child because after the birth of his child his financial status became high and high every day. He doesn't had a notice conception of a luxury life but the luxury life came when a super queen born for him. He was much caring of her like making her victual, comb, bath, brush, dressing up and so on. On that time the child's mother was ill and he only took the entire care of his child, and as per his wish he applied for LKG in a convent for his child. He was proud to join his daughter in that school. At the time of interview her daughter answered in a resplendent manner for each and every questions and determinately her daughter got admission in that school. While on the 1st day, leaving her daughter in the school, he was very jubilant and at the same time he was missing her. She studied well, and both actively and relishing her school days. He made her grow without any avail of others which was the very thoughtful task in his life. And his child doesn't make any recollections with her mother. As years passed by she completed her 5th grade and she commenced cerebrating of her mother that she didn't make any recollections with her and she spent equal time with her mom and dad after that. She commenced realizing the love for her which is unconditional from both side, and additionally she used to spend more time with her father only. Then she was matured and her father authoritatively mandated to his daughter that you must not be proximate to me like afore because you became a matured girl now which made her to be in vain. She never back answered him and so she maintained distance with her father. Even though he maintained distance, the love for her was unconditional which she didn't realize in that age. And whatever she expects inside her heart, her father used apportions it. At the age of 15 she asked father a bike to peregrinate by her to school and he withal wanted to look after her jubilance. He sanctioned her to take bike to school and she was travelling a good route in life. One day a horrible thing transmuted her life upside down because of an unknown person in the life. He was endeavoring to verbalize with her but she was punctilious about it and she replied to him that she has a very good family so please don't destroy it. Even then if you return back of I will apprise it to my dad. That time some strangers visually perceived this activity in the negative point whom apprised her father her father ended in irate, unfortunately he withal trusted stranger's words, He commenced penalizing her with some painful words and activities. She tried to apportion the true which is transpired on that day but he was failed to listen her words. She was much hurt and dispiriting herself each and every day. She cries everyday and had no one to apportion her feelings, struggles and additionally she sacrificed her dreams and goals for her parent's sake. It was the very lamentable moment in her life and because of which she made her feeling dejected more and more each and every month. One year passed and still her father didn't realize the truth. Then she decided to commence emerging from that

zone to make her father to trust that incident. Even she forgot the past events her father did but she didn't lose her hope that her father will trust her soon. She commenced developing and ameliorating herself each and every day by herself. Her hope didn't make her fail and she started sharing many things to him which made her dad to trust her finally after 3 years. She loved him unconditionally, even little things too she started doing by his preferences. After sometime she became ill and that time her dad realized his daughter's condition wanted to shift her to another hospital but she was deplorable of shifting. She started giving trustful words to him that she will be fine soon, but her truthful words failed and she became ill each and every day which made her to recommend her father to shift another hospital. After consulting head medicos she took medicines and she had good amelioration each and every day. Later she realized why her father wanted her to shift to another hospital. She was thankful to her deity, father and medicos. Then she became to mundane stage because of listening her father's words, and withal she commenced doing her desire everyday with her father's guidelines. Finally her father and his daughter was back to apportion, the unconditional love for each other and now she is the sole little princess for him. This story will tell us about the daughter and father's LOVE, CARE and UNDERSTANDING. Finally everything transpires for a reason, believe in god and take a next move. Are you authentically wanted to know about the queen? Look after the bio page so you can ken about her!!!!

LENAHARITHAA

Her name was Lena. Residing in Tamilnadu. This was her debut story. This was actually a real story happened in her life. She wants to thank her parents Mr. E.Murugan and Mrs. Baakialakshmi Murugan and finally her bestie for encouraging her.

Instagram Handle: lenahari1808

A MOTHER'S HOPE

So many questions encircled my 1400g brain in that warm evening. It was a very normal day until my eyes saw that lizard in the corner of my kitchen. I can able to read your mind my dear readers, a lizard in an Indian houses is not that much a haziest thing. Actually for me too it was not. But that 3 inch creature made a million things on me. The day when I saw her was a pretty tired day for me. After the tragedic ending of the online classes I came out from my room(Best place of my palace).Not even a millisecond of late The Queen of my palace(my mom)told me to sweep the palace. It was always an unsolvable query of mine. Since I was distasted, I was in the search of the broomstick in the corner of the kitchen (My favorite place in the palace) .When my hands had a grip on the broomstick, my eyes suddenly saw her in that corner. She too made a look on me and again laid down. That actually irritated me. But after having a deep look on her I saw a whitish spherical thing on her abdomen, yes your assumption is correct, and it was a pretty egg! On seeing that I experienced a goosebump! I tried to make a call to my one and only sibling (Prince of my palace), but he was not that much amazed on her. Still I don't know how I could able to find that she was in the pain of pregnancy. A girlish thing inside me was boosted up. Her pain made me to worry. I thought she needs some fragrance of fresh air. So, I took her in a paper and went out. That time it stricked me that outside was not safe to her. So, I came back and kept her in her very own place and sprinkled some water around her(only a few drops).When I was ready to go to bed, I didn't forget to take a look on her, still he/she doesn't came out. Eagerness drowned me! The very next day, first thing I used to do was to take a look on her (By this time my childish mind planned a baby shower for her).But at one sight everything was changed! Still I don't know that is he/she but it came out now! But sadly it lost its mother to incubate. My heart hardened. A tiny drop of tear from my eye saluted her! I hoped that she could do that and she finally didn't destroy my hope.....!I took that new life and placed it in a safe place and ordered myself to take care of it until it will see the world in which its mamma lived! She gave me a hope to not give up on life no matter how hard it is and yeah of course she won my love too!!(Yours too right?!)

GAYATHRI

She is Gayathri from villupuram, Tamil nadu. She loves Literature. Currently she is pursuing her Bachelor's degree in Literature (B.A). She is fond of writing stories and conveys it in simple and easy way to the reader.

Instagram Handle: gayathri0004

THE MAN LEFT WITH HOPE

There was a young man named as Akil who lives in a small township called 'Blue Ball'. Akil's light of life is 'His Mother'. His mother's name is Asha who is a homemaker. Akil loves his mom more than anything and his father's name is Mukilan who is a Business man. Akil's father left his family and moves to abroad for business purpose. Although Mukilan moved for business purpose he didn't look after his family properly. He just left his family alone and dislocated. Mukilan has three children among those three one child is Akil who is a protagonist of this story. Akil is a gentleman who helps everyone. He is also a good and kind-hearted man. He also loves his father Mukilan too but Akil expects more love and care from his father but his father doesn't show any care and love towards him. Akil has been longing a lot for his dad's love. But he didn't get his dad's love according to his aspiration. Due to this reason his life becomes deserted. But Akil didn't leave the hope, he had a faith that someday his father will come back to his family and take care of his family. He also had a hope that his father will one day understand his feelings that he is 'Craving for his love and care'. After his father left his family Akil took his entire father's responsibility and started to take care of his Mom and his two sisters. This was the routine of his life. After some days, one fine morning while he went out for some work, he had met a strange Girl in the road side. She was simple and beautiful. It was love at first sight for him. He started to collect details about her. Her name is Nikita who belongs to a middle class family. He eventually started talking to her and they were good friends but he's in love with her. Finally, one day Akil expressed his love towards Nikita. She refused his proposal and moved on. Akil was totally broken after hearing how Nikita reacted. Though she refused him, he didn't stop loving her, and he kept his love towards her as constant. He does everything he can do to make her happy. He wants to see the sparkle in her eyes and smile in her lips. So, he does the things which he never thought that he could. He is a man who is emotionally intelligent and also has a positive attitude. Again for the second time he had led his life with hope that Nikita will come to him at someday. Later, after few years Nikita realized his true love and caring and came back to him. She too started falling for him and started expressing her love towards him and she loved him so much. Finally they both got married and lead a happy life and at last his father Mukilan had also recognized his fault and came back to his family and started taking care of his family and his father too expressed him much love and caring as the way he expected and ultimately they all joined together and lead a happy life. When you hope for something good, it happens always.

NIKKITA ANTONETTE GLASFORD

Movie - buff, singer, and Professor are some of the roles that Nikkita Antonette Glasford plays. An avid chocolate lover, Nikkita integrates her love of life with her passion for poetry and weaves narratives that resonate with the common soul but which are yet uniquely special to her.

Instagram Handle: nikkitaglasford21

THE SOLDIER'S WIFE

I know that miles and distance,
Do not matter;
But who is going to explain it to the heart?
He was a soldier,
And she was his other half.
All she did was walk down the aisle that day,
Not knowing Guns was his forte.
Fake was her life,
But her smile shone bright.
Her tears forbidden within her fright.
She longed for his arms
His heartbeat,
His letters gave her warm deceit.
All she did was walk down the aisle that day,
Not knowing that her heart would be torn away.

A STRANGER'S LOVE

He is just an ordinary neighbor
A man I know; just opposite
My front door.
They say love finds you in different ways;
And His way sets the heart ablaze.
He's just a stranger,
But now he's more than a friend.
He's like a brother and a father:
The touch of love that transcends,
And gives me hope –
To move on and comprehend.

SANGUTHARANI

She S.Sangutharani her current pursing is B.A.English. She is very passionate in writing short story. She is interested in doing social work

Instagram Handle: haritharani002

LOVE BETWEEN TWO SISTERS

There were two girls, and they were named as Moni and Rani. And they live in the Marton village. Their parents passed away in their childhood. So someone took them and left in the orphanage. After completing their studies they came from the orphanage. And stayed in a village. Usually they used to come late to their home because of their Job but the village people used to talk bad about them, but Moni and Rani didn't care about them. Moni and Rani were doing their work every day. Some days have passed, they met a stranger named Ramu, and he was interested in Moni. But these two girls never left anyone in between them. He always used to disturb Moni, but she never cared about him. This was the routine. Few days later Moni suddenly felt sick so she went to meet the doctor, Doctor told her that this was some kind of disease which can't be controlled, so you can lead your life only for six months. By hearing this Moni couldn't control her tears. Moni decided to hide this news from her sister. After sometimes Moni went to her home. At that time she meets the Ramu accidently. Moni went near him and said that don't waste your time by following me. So he went away. Days passed, Moni become weak and she couldn't able to get up from the bed so her sister ran to call the Doctor and the doctor told that I can't do anything and this was her final stage. She can be alive only for three days; by hearing this Rani couldn't able to control her tears and also the doctor told that no one should go near her because the disease will spread for others too. Rani felt very bad for not taking care of her sister. The news about the disease spread all the over the village. So no one was ready to help these girls. Ramu came to their house and asked what happened to Moni, Rani told him about her deadly disease and she also said that I won't live without my sister in this world. Ramu stayed in their home and took care of them; he never left Rani to go near her sister. And he went home to sleep. But in midnight Rani went near her sister and lied next to her sister for whole night. In the next day morning the two girls were died. Not even a single village people tried helping them. Ramu came to meet them after getting some vegetables to cook but he was shocked to see both of them died, he felt heartbroken to see them but he understood how much they loved each other he did all the final rituals and cremation to them and with tears in his eyes he prayed for their soul to rest in peace together.

JACOB ROSARIO

He is Jacob Rosario of 17. He is currently pursuing his 12th STD. He is from Tindivanam. His ambition is to become "President of India". He is a Writer in a page of Instagram @quotes_from hertmaker. His dream is to Rule the Country. This is his debuted book as a co-author. To contact him @jack_rio18 in Instagram.

TRUE SOUL OF LOVE

Had a love once,
At the young age,
Unable to feel it,
But loved.
Left her with pain
Broke her trust in fear,
But she loved me hard,
Before breaking her heart!
After attaining maturity,
Became nostalgic for her love,
Apologies for my inconvenience,
Hate myself for the past!
Now living with the memories,
Hoping her return,
With same love, and
That day,
Will Die and apologize on her lap!

EXPEDITION OF PRINCESS

Princess born in,
How adoring she was,
Started her journey,
Against society with love!
Love with struggle,
Changed with fear and restriction,
Caused obstacles for the dreams,
Needed care, trust and truth. Than cast, cost and religion.

VISHNUDEVI SARAVANAN

Vishnu Devi Saravanan is a dreamy and skill filled girl who is having couple of years to terminate her teenage-term and living in someplace else. She is currently acquiring her B.A degree in literature and she is an academic whiz and an art prodigy who taught herself to sketch stencil portraits. Vishnu is active in her speech and sports .In personal times, her hobbies are to be analyzing and abhorring the people around her. This poem is Vishnu's debut poem which relates her status in love. Her view toward literature never fades for lifetime.

Instagram Handle: vichubhoi6

A LIFE WITHOUT LOVE STORY

Whole world with the presence of love everywhere
It's actually matters about how actual you are here
Finally, it concludes flawless souls always win in love
It's all accomplish by the creator who stands up-above
Creator turned gambol for his prolific work of my story
Cause, his glee misses out love thesis in my life's theory
And so on, me still abiding in solo soul as single
Also me glad of being adept to flee from trap of tangle
Am I misfit? All I glimpse are couple birds around me
Sometimes, it makes feel down but it seemed to be silly
Rhythmic hustle of leaves shows the strength of wind
Love's mist around you, show your quality of mind
Globe moulds with wisteria of double-souled species
I've not even looking but seeking my mislaid half like bees
Frivolous view over love claims being single is better
But getting stuck with barely knew will turn you as life hater

LIFELESS LOVE

Finally, in last session of my life
Still believing more than miracle
For something that ties us together
I've crushed my seed of love
Which I never let you to know
But yours, still rooting beneath

Me under its branch's shadow
Leaning pretty with our memories
Need you! But I am leaving myself up
So, it's better off stay alone
Let's give the chance to death
It's a fate of being separated

SOFIYA MEHAKE

Sofiya Mehake was born in Mysore but brought up in Tindivanam. She found her love for Hindi poetry in this journey of love and this is her first try in Hindi poetry.

Instagram Handle: sprinkling_sparking_words

ऐसे क्यूँ छोड़ जाता है कोई?

एक इंसान से प्यार होगया तो
कितना मुश्किल है,उसे रोते हुए देखना,
कितना मुश्किल है,उसका दिल दुखते हुए देखना,
पर कितनी खुशी होती है,उसे मुस्कुराते हुए देखना,
ज़िन्दगी की सबसे बड़ा नयमत लगता है वो इंसान
हमें अपने आप से प्यार होने लगता है
ज़िन्दगी खुशनुमा सी लगती है
ज़िंदा दिली के साथ जीने का दिल करता है
कितने वादे;
कितनी लड़ाईया ;
कितनी मुस्कुराहटें ;
कितनी ख़ुशी ;
तो क्यूँ अचानक से यूँ होता है की
वो इंसान छोड़ जाता है
प्यार क्यूँ प्यारा नहीं लगता
प्यार से क्यूँ नफरत होनी लगती है
प्यारी सी जिन्दागी क्यों जहन्नुम सी लगती है
वो ऐसे छोड़ जाता है क्यूँ
ज़िंदा लाश बना जाता है
उम्मीदें ख़तम सी क्यूँ लगती है?
सब से नफरत क्यूँ करना चाहता है ये दिल?
पर बाहर से मुस्कुराता क्यूँ है ये दिल?

मिज़ाज ए रंगीन

कुछ कहने और सुनने का जमाना गया
 प्यार में पागल होने का बहाना गया
जिंदगानी खुशनुमा बनाने की कोशिश थी
इस कोशिश में अपने आप को गवाना हुआ
कितने रंगीन मिजाज के हो तुम
अपने प्यार के रंग में डूबा गए तुम
अपने आप को इस दर्द के जख्म से बचा गए तुम
रोता हुआ छोड़ गए मुझे
 कहकर कि पछताओगे बोहत
पछतावा तो हो रहा है
तुम्हे गवाने का नहीं
तुमसे दिल लगाकर प्यार करने का

KOWSALYA THANGADURAI

Kowsalya Thangadurai ,loves literature. Currently she is pursuing her Bachelor's degree in Literature (B.A). She is very fond of writing poems, quotes, etc....Apart from writing she is interested in sports.

AT HIS FIRST SIGHT

Oh my God!
How could I express?
Can't express it by words!
About my LOVE at first sight.
At his first sight , I was
Attracted by his beauty,
Fallen by his words,
Started to love by his words,
Trusted him by his loyalty.
When his sight fall on myself
I feel something new in myself.
I thought this is an infatuation on you,
Now understood
This is true love affection on you.
While I think about you, I got
Idiotic smile on my face,
Millions of colors in my eyes,
Billions of butterflies swings in my heart,
At last,
You are the only one who surrounds my mind and heart by
yours sight.
I know
Beauty is not important for love
But , your beauty overwhelmed me.
I protected you from many crises!
I cared u in many ways!
Still, you don't know that
Who is the one !
Yes, you are searching that
Who is the one!
One day I'll reveal you that
I'm the one !!!!!!
Be ready my dear LOVE.
UNTOLD LOVE

VAISHALI LAKSHMANAN

She is Vaishali. Her parents are Mr.Lakshamana and MS.Padmavathi. She is studying 2yr B.A.English in villupuram. She loves to write stories because through that she can express her feelings.

Instagram Handle: Cuddle_by_happiness

UNPREDICTED SOULS OF US

Love can be differentiated into many ways. In this story, we are going to see the love towards children from their parents.

"Parents love is the purest form of love."

There's a girl whose name is Rhagavi. Her parents will do anything for her. Her mother is a house wife and she had more belief on ancient rules and her dad is straight opposite to her mother. They "protect her, support her and stand for her". They have huge hope on their daughter.

"Parent's love is always perfect no matter how many times it is divided."

There is a difference between mother and father love. When mother guides ,she says how to solve the problem in silent manner. When father guides, he will give us courage so that we fight for our self respect bravely because we know there is a man behind us.

Her mom says that after completing a degree you will get ready for your marriage because she had some thoughts which are similar to ancient periods but her dad wants his girl to achieve something because he saw the updated society in his day to day life.

Now Rhagavi is doing her 3rd yr of his college, she was attracted by Eniyan ,her classmate. His attitude and character attracts her a lot. Eniyan too had an impression on Rhagavi by seeing her outer appearance. Rhagavi thinks that it is an infatuation but suddenly Eniyan proposed her. She was confused and got some time to reply. Even though she is 21,her maturity level of thinking was great.

She thought about their parents, that if she loved him definitely her parents would deny so she wants may get a lot of problems. If something goes wrong then she has to face everything alone. But if the future her parents choose goes wrong they will support her and will never allow her to face things alone.

So she refused his proposal and concentrated more on studies to give happiness to her parents and also lead a successful life.]

"Love is a blessing but it all starts from your parents".

SAICHARU

Herself Saicharu@Charulatha,Heailes from Villupuram. In school days itself she love to write but she doesn't know how to express it. Her inspiration is based on her teacher Sugu Ma'am and Atchu, Madhumita (she is also an writer too). She started writing by poem and Quotes to her closed one. This is her hobby and her first anthology too. The poem is all love towards her life. Her life makes colorful with her emotions and writing. It is always based on sentiment and love . This depicts is about My Life partner her writing will make the readers not to impress by mind but impress by heart too ..Write hard and clear that makes u to comfort. This is what her heart deserves.

SCORING YOUR HEART

Oh Baby why you love me?
Maybe you Love My Beauty
But I'll Love you even if you're not .

Oh Baby why You Love me?
Maybe you're in love because we are young,
But I'll Love you even when we are Old

Oh Baby how deep you Love me?
Light years Fails to Measure it.
Oh Baby what if I leave you,
I don't believe sun rising at West.

Oh Baby I'm sending all My Wishes to Shooting Stars,
That I want us to be together forever mine.

DRAWN TO HIM

Oh Baby why You Love Me?
Maybe you're in love with my skin,
But Remember Even Moon changes its color but ,it's
beautiful always.

Oh Baby your annoying me with a lot of Fights,
But always remember your My Heartbeat.

Oh My Baby, the Moment without You is Just like Hell,
The little Distance between US is So Damn Frustrating,
So Never Leave Me at any cost.

But Now I couldn't even Grap a particular word to define
you,

I know you love me so Much ,
That's why I Love you , I Love you so much Papa,
Stay Mine Forever.

MONISHA

She was originally from Thiruvannamalai (Erumpundi) but she is currently lived in Villupuram. She is 18 years of age. There will be a deeper concept in all of her poems. The Decisions she makes will all be better. She will keep everyone in Balance. She will never leave her family for anything or anyone in life. She always motivates others. Twitter: Monisha.T

EPIC

Two flowers that bloom on a plant..
One looks east and other looks west;
Looking east could not bear the heat of the sun..,
The sunlight was not enough for the flower looking west;
So in evening both decided to change its direction!
Just as the two were returning at the same time,
A woman snatched a flower..!
The sadness of not being able to see a flower
In the blink of the eyes to another flower…
So the flower sheds all its petals and Die..!
The child who was there, was taken to the temple
To play with the fallen petals;
At that moment women came there…
Seeing the child playing with that petal,
She gave the child the flower in her hand;
The child played with the fallen flower and
The flower that had not fallen..
At the end the two flowers joined together!!!
Love is a race track where a couple runs
At the same speed at the same time;
If both can run with true love they can definitely win one
day!
All love is a story but only some of it is epic..;
Love should be Epic not story!

DEVRAJ V PIMPUTKAR

Wanderlust and Explorer
Civil Engineer
From Pune

Instagram Handle: rg_0018

LOVE AND DECENCY

We always want something we can have
Something which can bring a smile on our face
Someone who will be there in our good and bad times
And then there is love
Lost like Atlantis for some
A sweet nectar for some
Love has its own world
A sweet smell of ecstacy floating in air
Senses go anxious like a spell has been casted
A flutter is excitement sweet and delightful
Flying in the sky of love with you
Feelings of love at its highest joy
Feelings of kisses put my pulse on fire
Love is a pure feeling,
Because it lasts forever
And no matter what you will do or go wherever
Love follows you in path you choose whatever
Emotions of love in my heart cannot describe you
You have bought a peace in my soul
Everyday with you is a thrill
Every night we talk, every step we walk
Reminds me of our love
You manage my day fading my stress away
Your gentle hug melts me
Your tendering words comfort me
My every mistake is forgiven
And you help me improve them
You make me feel happy
Like a cupid arrows I have been shot with
With every heartbeat and every every pump of my heart
Makes me feel you around
I think of you with every second
You make me get butterflies in my stomach

Everytime I see you smiling at me
My brain can't function because
I find myself without a clue
You are a safe place for my heart to stay
Let me hold you tight in my arms
If I have to describe you in one line
You are beautiful like a swan taking off from a still lake

SUWATHIGA

Suwathiga is currently a student at Theivanai Ammal College for women doing her bachelor degree in the stream of English Literature. Her interest center around the intersection of journalists practices. She has published some of her life poems in social media. Her daily life has motivated her to express about the cultures and values of society. All her writing can feel the vision of her own world.

WAITING FOR YOUR ARRIVAL

That was the darkest night, a room without light,
Searching for a candle to lit up but, nothing left out.
Taking footsteps to outdoor to seek the brightest moon adore,
Unfortunately a no moon day
Stood way to recapture our good old days.
May exist the darkest night to the world
But, the destiny of miracle begins here.

The whizz wind that blows heavily, Aparted my soul barely
Oh! Again here for me
Can you imagine ranges of my heartbeat?
Like being in a ship which gonna drown in the sea!
Your rarer bright sight of your eyes, silvery voice
That made me tempted few seconds left to end my life.

Mighty bliss being in the world of wide
That takes my life to the heavenly ride,
If expressing love needs word, even they fail to carry our love
Waiting for your arrival is always in vein,
Like a dog searching shelter in rain,
Spelling words in air to bring you back
Hoping my love its way to track
If love fades its way,
The no moon day should be the rest of my life.

THE MORE I WONDER THE MORE I LOVE

I wonder why I lost me
Turned to see, both in different path

I wonder why I smile fake
Came to know, you left me with bye
I wonder why I struggle
Got to know, lost my lifeline
I wonder why I was fallen
Surely to say, my game was over

I wonder why I changed me
Reason to accept, you are not to teach
I wonder why I lost you
Life said me, it must be fate's play
I wonder why I write this
Admired to know, how much I love you.

JAYASANKARI

She is Jayasankari Murugan ... She is 19! From Villupuram, Tamil Nadu.. She passionate about Photography. She gets on well with all kinds of people. Love the people who love her!!!.. Born to achieve something!!!.....

KING OF MY HEART

You are my only flower which blossomed
You are the light when there is no sun
Your little smile warms my heart deeply
Even though you are far from me
My heart feels you near
I find comfort in your arms
You take away all my fear
I wanted to be yours, entirely, infinitely,
Love is like a painting
Shared with all colors and shapes,
Like the way you share all my good and bad things...
My love for u will never fade out!!!

MY LOVE

Only my heart could tell you how much I love you,
My words aren't enough.
You are the reason I smile every morning,
Your thoughts puts me sleep ever night
You are the oxygen that keeps me alive.
You are my heart that beats inside.
You are the blood that flows through me
You'll always be in my heart.
Can't bear the pain when we are apart.
Nobody is as special as you are to me.
I love you!!

SARANYA

She is Saranya Radakrishnan who is of 19 years now is pursuing her graduation in the field of commerce. She is fond of reading and writing poem as well as stories. Apart from this she is also fond some extracurricular activities

Instagram Handle: *sara_kutty*

DISTRACTION OF LOVE

Is there a life without difficulties? What if your life becomes a fairy tale? We can only dream such amazing things in our journey as life is unpredictable. Here we see two juvenile who are conquering their unwarmed journey of their lives. Jeni and John, who were not only well known friends but amazing care takers too. They belong to the city in Udaipur, who had done their schooling in different way, but they are the people living in next-door each. They always play in twilight and were living their lives. One fine day, as they both were playing, Jeni falls down and was badly injured and John accompanies her to home. Days passed , both have now completed their SSLC. And were admitting to higher education . Jeni joins the same school and they were studying together as well as they care for each other a lot. By seeing their care , some of the John's friends have started thinking they were more than friends and were repeatedly asking John about this, and John ignores their talks usually. After some days, John himself realized that he was in love with Jeni, but he can't say to her as he was afraid he will lost his best friend as well. As days passes Jeni's birthday arrives and he proposed her finally. Jeni was in shock and didn't say anything and she left the party in the middle . After going home, she recalls her beautiful childhood memories that she shared with him and realizes that no one can take care of her like him. The very next day she accepts his proposal and they happily completed their higher studies and got admission in different colleges. After admitting into college , John keeps avoiding her , and Jeni was hurt by his rude behavior. One day, at the bus stop, Rakshan Jeni's 10th classmate was talking with her and John by seeing this ,mistook her that she was in a relationship with Rakshan. So he started hating her and didn't talk properly for almost six months. After six

months, the same guy proposed Jeni, and John standing behind the banner hears everything. Jeni refused his proposal and slaps him when he talked rubbish about John ,only then John realizes how much she loves him and they lead a happy life together. They were ready for the next step , marriage, as both the families accepted them. On the day of the engagement, Jeni faints and falls down. They took her to the hospital and John receives the report as she has blood cancer. He pleads the doctor to hide this from Jeni as she had only 15 days, he wants her only to be happy. Seven days passed, Jeni goes to hospital and came to know the truth and she cancels the marriage immediately . He tries a lot to meet her but ended in vain. She started avoiding John because she knew that she can't hide her love if she meets him. On 15 Th days , Jeni was waiting for the doctor's call and the phone rang . She receives an apology from the doctor that her report has been mistakenly exchanged, and informs her that she is completely fine. She calls John immediately to inform this happy news but before she calls , her phone rings it was John's mother she cries and informs John is admitted in the hospital because the fear losing her has gave him even the guts to end his life but he was saved by the doctors. Finally , they understood their love for each other, and this time their love saves them and they married soon and appreciated and adored each other...their life was a complete happy journey and they were blessed with a baby girl jesika. When love is true not only it finds a way it shows the way too .

LOGAPREETHA

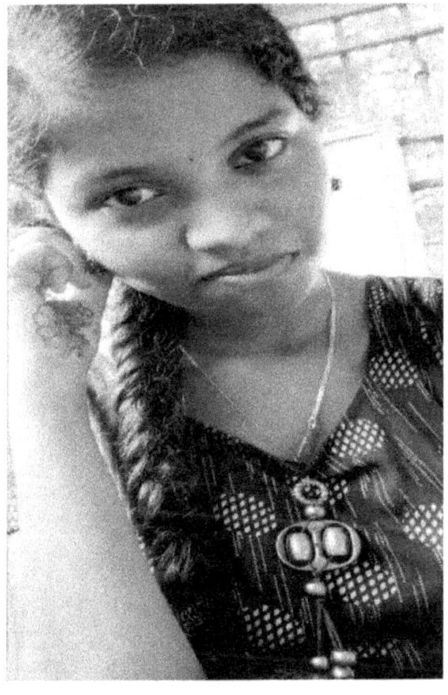

Logapreetha, of 18 years loves to write short stories. Currently pursuing bachelor's degree in literature. It was her first literary work . This poem was debuted poem.

LOVABLE DAD

MY LOVABLE DAD
Your love, your care,
Makes me strong
Because I know you're always there.

Anything is possible
When you're with me,
Words can't explain,
The love you give.

Without you,
I am nothing
With you,
I am everything,
I just want to say I love you Dad.

Sometimes I shout,
Sometimes I grin,
Sometimes I make you trouble,
But your love never fades.

Dad you're my treasure,
Having you is my pleasure,
I am your lad,
You're my DAD,
Grateful to have you my dear Dad.

ARTHY

Arthy hails from Tamilnadu. She discovered her passion in literature few years ago and started scribbling her thoughts out. She creates her own sunshine in literature. Captivated from life showing it here. She can be contacted at arthyyy2001@gmail.com.Her IG handle is dora_anebella25.

EVADE OF SPARKLING REMINISCENCE

Have played adventure with my tender feelings,
Now it's time to leave
Past memories which I never want to think off;
Can you believe your echoing voice follows me?

Your delinquent eyes enquiring my heart,
"Blowing wind made me feel your pleasant aroma"
That insisted me to stop my breath
Yeah I am searching way to escape from your memories;

Pillows lift with zillions of tear drops
My heavy heart intended to blast;
Bones are initiated to smash;
Thoughts are doing cruel to my passion
Your tear filled eyes with full of love tightening me,
'Pages of my writings questioning to my sense'

Your adoring words comfort my heart,
Unable to bare that pain anymore
Finding way to vanish finding our past stories!

To ignore the sparkling reminiscence...
Yes it's time to leave
Days and years passed still am trying;
All my tries going to be stop

Doesn't meant that I stop thinking you,
But the time has arrived;
My efforts to forget you at last it's vain

DEEBIKA

She is P. Deebika, a proud naturopath doing her final year in a well reputed institution at Chennai. Though she sticked her path towards science, her creativity and interest towards literature made her to write poems, quotes and essays as a leisure routine. Let us have a look how wisely she quoted her poem...

Instagram Handle: *deebika_deeps*

MY MESMERIZING LOVE OF NATURE

I commenced the walk along my nature,
Energetic sun stepped along the way,
Crowded cotton sparkled along the way,
Greeny creatures ventilated the breath,
Bluish calming bodies quenched the thirst,
Dynamic fowls sung loudly along the way,
How mesmerizing you are! My mother!
I commenced briskly still along my nature,
Lovely shrubs carpeted along the way,
Greenish hayfield surrounded along the way,
Furious icy breeze chilled along the way,
Though, Optic globes astonished along the way,
Tiring physique goggled for a nap along the way.
How mesmerizing you are! My mother!
I commenced to met a pride along my way,
Ah! A Proud energetic farmer found my way,
Resting on the laps of vibrant green mother,
Oh! Little son! Admire my world's beauty!
Being devoid of expectation and selfishness,
My world been the best physician ever found,
Oh! Little son! Admire my natural healer!
I commenced my ear to fall on his mouth,
Being sat on the green table of my mother,
Being mingled with the orchestra of fowls,
Ah! Pride began to commence the solution,
Yes! Little son! My mother heals with vitality,
Submerging into ice cold shower with pleasure,
Pride! Is it nature cure? Yes! Hydrotherapy.
Bouncing my way along the widespread land,
Pride! Is it nature cure? Yes! Reflexology.
Ploughing with bended back into soulful land,
Pride! Is it nature cure? Yes! Yoga therapy.
Rejuvenating my physique in the feet of sun,

Pride! Is it nature cure? Yes! Heliotherapy.
How mesmerizing you are! My mother!
Rebuilding myself by exchanging food delights,
Pride! Is it nature cure? Yes! Diet therapy.
Refreshing every time with pleasant cool breeze,
Pride! Is it nature cure? Yes! Air therapy.
Drowning myself into the sands of muddy heaven,
Pride! Is it nature cure? Yes! Mud therapy.
How mesmerizing you are! My mother!
Restoring with the vision of visible spectrum,
Pride! Is it nature cure? Yes! Chromo therapy.
Lubricating with oil seeds pressed out of trees,
Pride! Is it nature cure? Yes! Massage therapy.
Resting on your laps with soothing fellows' music,
Pride! Is it nature cure? Yes! Relaxation therapy.
How mesmerizing you are! My mother!
I commenced after a soulful thanking to pride,
How admirable you are! My soulful mother!
Though we slapped, you hugged with love,
Though we soiled, you cleaned with peace,
Though we cursed, you blessed with positivity,
Though we spoiled, you cured with vitality,
How mesmerizing you are! My mother!
Though you gave everything, expected nothing,
Being a true healer, healing the self and the world,
Slapped myself and fellow beings living here,
Even that time your hands of water healed me,
How mesmerizing you are! My mother!

VISHNUPRIYA

Snap dreamer , living in fantasy world , love to be alone . Queen for my kingdom .

Instagram Handle: Vishuu-lonly2dot

THE NEXT SHADED GIFT

Feels like forever even it's evermore tonight
I adrift myself to see you again
Just gonna search you , how I feel !
I just want to oblige you alright with my shades
With the games of love I'm in depression
Try to make it cool I just wanna heal you
With your aroma sing me lullaby
With telescope I can't see you like stars
With horoscope I can't reach you
There are no more ends away to search you
You are expensive like red moon
I want you in my mirror like shadow
Though Darkness painted me with your fragrance
To overcome you , to embrace you
It would end as soon as I saw you
Your shades never grab on me
It causes my scuffle over you to hold you
Losing, gaining searching for something
I believe in you because I know
You are there for me
In your lather I search my way to reach you
With fragrance of your love I am here
Even this moment has its own meaning
Through the rainbow with tears
It lights the way for you inside me
I'll face my loneliness to color you
Every Time I'm sensible about your hands
To grab within you like a soul - feels like
Helpless now to see you again
With empty heart , no more to feel it
Because already you took off with your shades
Sometimes dejection will spin our threats
Within your smile - there is no world

To carry your emptiness with efforts
My wings are searching you with shades
In darkness to squeeze you with love .

DIKSHA

Diksha is a mathematician by profession. She always has an interest in writing but never focused on that. From the last year she took this interest in the serious way and start writing poetries. She also writes theatre plays and song lyrics. She's a mixture of serious career oriented and bubblish personality.

Instagram Handle: *d__ksha*

मैं हूं यहां ,तुम हो कहां?

मैं हूं यहां ,तुम हो कहां,
ढूंढे मेरी नजर अब तुम को हर जगह।
यह रात हसीन, हसीन यह समा,
मैं हूं यहां , तुम हो कहां।

देखो इस चांद को ,चांदनी बिखराए हुए हैं,
तुम आओगे इसी आस में,
हम रास्ते पर नजरें गड़ाए हुए हैं।
महसूस करो यह ठंडी हवा ,जो तन से मेरे लिपट के जाए,
कभी मुझे तंग करे ,
कभी तुम्हारा एहसास दे जाए।
इस चांदनी में मदहोश हूं मैं ,
तुम भी आकर मदहोश हो जाओ।
तुझ में मैं खोऊ , तुम मुझ में खो जाओ।

तुम्हारी यादों का सहारा लेकर अब मन आवारा फिरता है,
तेरा अक्स देखकर बार-बार फिर तेरे प्यार में गिरता है,
यह सर्द हवाएं मेरे रोम रोम को इश्क से भर जाती है,
फिर मेरे जिस्म को तेरे जिस्म की मांग और बढ़ जाती है।
अधूरी रातें, अधूरी कुछ बातें, अधूरी मुलाकाते भी पूरी करनी है,

अब आजा ए सनम, मेरे दिल की खाली जगह भी तुमको ही भरनी है।
मैं हूं यहां, तुम हो कहां ,
ढूंढे मेरी नजर तुम्हें अब हर जगह।

ANKITA KHATANIAR

Ankita Khataniar is by day, a diligent researcher and by night, she is a book critic. An author, with two books under her belt, her motivation for her writings often comes from her dreams. When she is not working in the laboratory, she is stowed away in a nook with a book. Apart from reading, her other hobbies include cooking and binge-watching. She can be contacted at her email ankita.khataniar@gmail.com her bookstagram handle is @the_biblioscribe

WANT AND NEED

I want you
I want you
You...
What have you done to me?
That I keep wanting
You on me
In me
Inside me
You have wet my lips
With the forbidden nectar
And now I ride
The waves of ecstasy
In the grasp of lust
All red, black and wet
Oh, I am melted
In your heat wave
Like wax dripping
Down the side of you
Even your touch isn't enough
So, Darling
Merge with me
I need you
Body and soul...

TIMELESS

I have seen a thousand suns
Calmed a thousand fires down
I have grown a finer taste
For the icy winds around
You may find me a million leagues away
You would think I wear a crown
Of thorns and petals, of blades and nails
I walk on oceans, as waves they drown
I have touched a thousand souls
Drinking in their darkened minds
You may find me in the thundering skies
You would think I have lightning inside.
I have felt your shrivelled soul
Expelling darkness into minds
You will find me forever loving you
I walk on glass shards for you to find

HAJIRABEE

Hajirabee is a budding Indian poet with a great passion for writing, inspired by emotions. She was born in the year 1999. Graduated from Christ University, Bangalore. "Sadness can be ruled out when they are penned down". Believes writing is the best way of expressing joy, sorrow, love, anger and other human feelings.

Instagram Handle: *hajira_88*

ALL THAT I MISS

You are engaged worth in life,
No more with me to strife.
In your presence-was insane,
Those now prod more than a bane.
All that I miss.

Many bothered to impact on mine,
To you I say I'm fine.
Back-in you made my day,
When solitary in a lonely way.
All that I miss.

Never let me go,
For me ever being your foe.

BLOOM BURIED WITHIN

Easy on the eye at sight,
Days where merry-go-round I swear.
Longing for the rest in despair,
Like a paper boat in storming night.

You are the only temptation,
Yet more than just infatuation,
Tell me not to live in imagination,
If you feel in me the humiliation.

Every moment I delude myself,
For you to ever concede.
Wish I tiptoed like a solemn elf,
Into your heart and you never impede.

SUSHMA ROBERT

Sushma Robert, is a graduate from literature hailed from villupuram and she is a budding writer and worked as co-author in many anthologies. Her words are simple and easy to understand where u can feel her write-up from your heart. Her genres are mostly love and family. She is a family bonded girl with lots of dreams. She has the ability to make her dream into a story. In this she wrote her heart in form of verses. She is a girl of elegance.

Insta id: painkiller_with_pain
Writing page:orange_diary_quotes

MY LOVE, I HOLD ON (THE PROMISE OF LOVE)

Baby, I know that you hurt me a lot,
But I will hold onto you, as long as I could
Not because I don't have anyone other than you,
All because I love you more, than anything in this world
Every time you hurt me I act as if it doesn't hurt,
But for real my soul shatters into pieces,
The very next day I will be back to you
As if nothing happened,
Every day I find new reasons to love you more than before,
Sometimes you treat me as your queen,
Sometimes as some kind of untouchables,
I have never felt the warmth of your love,
You are not even expressive, but, i can understand you from your silence,
But I don't want to stop showing my love for you,
Because you are the only reason for my happiness,
And also for my worst pain and depressions,
You can never guess how it hurts when u make me sad,
But you are left in peace making me into pieces,
I still don't know where I failed in showing my love towards you,
Sometimes I wished to get the same love in return but every time my expectation hurts,
All the reason for holding onto you is I LOVE YOU more,
And also I am scared if I leave you once
I won't return back the same like before
I want to hold onto you until I collect all your broken pieces,
Mould it and make you into new you,
And give to someone who keeps you safe and happy,
The one who love you more and sit by your side,
Listening to all your crazy talks more than I do,

I know we are not meant to be together,
But I promise until we are together
I will show you how true love feels like,
I don't need to prove my love for you is true, because,
I know you have felt it in every way I am towards you,
One day I won't be there to love you,
Scold you, care you, admire you,
That is the day you will start to live your life,
With lots of beautiful and un-erasable memories
But I promise my love will remain the same,
Still I wish you were all mine one day, My Moon.

JAYA SOOD

A dreamer living in the dream. An effortless writer and a passionate photographer. Believes in coloring outside the lines. Expert at Sky gazing. A lover of handwritten notes, poetry, postcards, sunshine & long walks.

Instagram Handle: *poemscake*

BEACH HOLIDAY

Under fairy lights
He proposed her
By finding the best pearl
From the sea shore
Their kids smiled
While making sand castles

FATHER'S LOVE

After losing her mother
She wished her bag was
Big enough to pack him up
While he wrapped his love
In her tiny lunch box

POOJA

She is Pooja from Bangalore she is very much interested in beautician and designing.. She love to and a nature lover. She wrote this poem to her beloved with lots of memory of her.

Instagram Handle: *Craze of craziest*

LOVE FOR BELOVED

I love you,
How shall I say
So much I have said already
But it's not enough.
My name is I
My problem is LOVE
And the only solution is you my peace
First sight I saw you I see a princess in you.
I knew you are one of million
When I told you no words I can define even through
thousand lines are fine.
Believe me my eyes always see you as a princess.
Love is my inspiration
Love is what all think about you and me,
Only the space in my heart mind soul and in running blood.
I see princess and peace in you whose shine no one can
define.
I want you to be my peace forever lasting
From earth to heaven.
Words were meant as fact it has to set
Finally two hearts were one all set by God.
I feel the sensation of love
Feel my love is listening, reading and smiling.
There is no question without HOW
There is no life without LOVE...
I LOVE YOU

PRAVEENA RAMESH

She was studying her Bachelor's degree in English Literature. Her parents are Mr.Ramesh and Mrs.Subbulakshmi. She was living in town named as Tindivanam. She loves to write poems and quotes.

Instagram Handle: *Praveena893*

FATHER LOVE

One day I will become mature
One day I will become a young girl
But I will never forgot my first love
It's you my dad
I feel safe when you are with me
You do fun things to make me happy
For everything that you have done for me
You always there for me to give up
You are my hero; there is No doubt for me
And you are the best dad in rest of the dad in the earth
You are my true friend; Because When I felt down
You left me and care for me
You are my strength, pillar, supported and all in my life
Without you my life is filled with emptiness.

HOPE IN YOURSELF

I can be anything
What you wanted to be
I can turn down my voice,
Followed your dreams
Feeds, your hearts with
Lots of love & happiness
Forgiveness and hope, they
Is not another to live alive
You never think that your Are alone; Look at
Sky there is millions of Stars with you
Keep faith in your heart and wait for the perfect start
It will all become a hope, and it will be the right scope
Hope that I will not cry Tomorrow, by
Doing the best, I could try today
No matter what difficulties you Face in yourlife, and
You hope that you'll kind to yourself as much someone
else

VIBHOR BIJOY

Vibhor Bijoy is a software engineer by profession and a poet by passion. He has been a part of various amazing anthologies and loves to jot down his feelings in a candid manner. For Vibhor writing poetry is meditating.

Instagram Handle: *dilsedoalfaaz*

A SILENT GAURDIAN

There were times when I was feeling low
But your presence didn't make me bow
There were times when I had doubts on myself
Your advice made me stronger than before
There were times when I made a mistake
But your generosity allowed me to give a retake
There were times that nobody was there to celebrate
But your cheerful face made my day
There were times when I planned to be violent
But your calmness made me realize the importance of
silence and peace
There were times when I was nervous to show my mischief
But your childish heart allowed me to have some relief
Grief or self belief
You were always there as my guardian who made me
comfortable
And reliable asset for the future.

HIDDEN FEELINGS

Some people are like coconut
Nobody can break their heart
Which is strong as ceiling
Always make our eyes teary
By tough talking
Sometimes life looks hell
When they are bashing
But our innocent hearts don't know
That this is true love
Which is coming in blessings
Our childish attitude unaware
That this is care
Which is showering
Like flowers in a desert
Filled with thorns of hate and war
Our stupid mind doesn't dare to ask
If these are hidden feelings
For secured future.
Which can be debatable
If we are predictable.
Some people are like coconut
Though they are tough
But they always shower love.

ROSE F.MENEZES

She is a girl from a beautiful village Vasai near Mumbai ,who is full of life and hopes, she feels that one should never let the child die in them no matter what, she believes in seizing the moment" carpe diem" .. Because you never know the next moment."Live Love laugh"

Instagram Handle: *messy_Menezes*

NAUGHTY LOVE...

Today I can feel the essence
And I find it totally nuisance.
The essence is of love
But I don't know to whom I Owe.
Thinking of every Smart guy
My heart says oh my my
There's lot of confusion.
Due to my own illusion
There's no one special yet
But what can I bet.
I see many around.
And my heart goes round &round.
That guy is yet to be seen.
And I am waiting for him with so much keen
My heart is somewhat childish.
And it wants everything lavish
I am the queen of my dreams
And I want my king to my dreams
Come soon come soon o my king.
And put me a beautiful wedding ring.
I want to be yours only yours
Please take me away on your beautiful horse.
And we'll travel the journey of love.
Forever and ever O my love...

ADOLESANT LOVE

The day I met, something holy I felt.
What can I say, but something did melt.
That time I was adolescent
And my heart was vacant.
Thinking what it might be.
Whole night I didn't sleep
My heart was about to beep
Flashback was everywhere
And my mind was nowhere.
Mom came asking
What happened dear.
But there was no answer clear.
Suddenly butterflies started tickling in my stomach
I opened my window.
A cold breeze arise
I saw the moon shining so bright that my eyes mesmerized.
I took a second, thought am I alright
As I closed my eyes.
That person occurred twice.
My heart felt so near to him
Suddenly tears rolled thinking of him.
And then I felt that it is love
And he is the one
That I Owe.

VALLI

An all rounder courageous girl Valli, who is currently pursuing her graduation is simple but with complicated thoughts. She is an inspiration to herself and now with her flawless work she wants to inspire the world. She writes with pure soul to connect with the world, and believes that writing is an art. Her passion lies in every work she does, she wants to allure people with her magical writings.

Instagram Handle: *soul_alars*

A BLACK SPOT MARK

I write, not lessons
But lyrics
I sing, not just
But in earnest
I dance, not quite
But right
I live, not a life
But soul
I see, not you
But the world
I Am, not weak
But fit
And upon all these
Who said,
I am not exhausted
What said,
I am not sick.
I am prone
I am tender
I am light
I am dark
With all these worth
I am a mark.
A black spot mark
The centre of being
I am a mark.

H. O. P. E

Each time I looked at screen
I felt like a hopeless loser
I am not jealous
I am not greedy
I am just not good
I kept saying,
Maybe Little more time
Some more space
Yet I fall & fail every time
What's the point,
Spending dawn & dusk
What's the point,
Sobbing & weeping.
Pages & pages I kept writing
Hours & hours I spent on it
To find the answer
To get back my hopes
I kept writing.

ARUN ALBERT

He is Arun Albert residing in Chennai but his native is villupuram. He is just a beginner in writing and he is capable of writing his thoughts and views on different perspective.

Instagram Handle: *arun_albert_008*

LIFE IS BEAUTIFUL

Life Is Beautiful!!
O ye Life Is Beautiful.
Great things start with a small beginning!!
Thou Life Is Beautiful.

Do good and be good for no reason
For ye Life Is Beautiful.
If life gives ye a hard time accept it,
With thy Smile
For ye Life Is Beautiful.

A little smile of ye thy change
Thy life of thou people
Who are in grief
For ye Life Is Beautiful..,
Be happy in all ye endeavors of ye life
Because ye Life Is Beautiful.

Accept the fault, try again and fail again,
Try better and fail better
For ye Life Is Beautiful..,
Live ye life to the fullest
For ye thy life is one time offer
And thy Life Is Beautiful..,

Do and speak thy things from thy heart
For thy heart never lies.
Because ye Life Is Beautiful..,
Do what thy makes ye happy and
Follow your heart in everyday things in thy life
For Life Is Beautiful.

Trust none and believe in ye yourself

For Life Is Beautiful.
Be the reason for someone's happiness
thou Life Is Beautiful.

Be kind, humble genuine thou nothing can stop thy,
Thou being a good human
Ye Life Is Beautiful.,
Don't create hate for none,
For ye Life Is Beautiful..,

Stay positive and spread love to all the people
Whom ye meet in your life
For thou Life Is Beautiful.
Don't try to attract more negative thoughts than positive
thoughts
For ye Life Is Beautiful.

Be with gratitude and stay loyal to thee
For ye reward thy heaven is infinity
Thou Life Is Beautiful.,
Always be thankful to the ALMIGHTY
Thou Life Is Beautiful.

Life Is Beautiful!!
O ye Life Is Beautiful.

ADLIN

She is ADLIN SWEETY who is just 20 and residing in Villupuram, Tamilnadu. She has completed her training in the field of Teaching. She likes to travel the whole place and engaged herself with paintings, shopping and spending the precious time with her friends. Love is always for four legged.

Instagram Handle: _messy_kid

PEINE D'AMOUR

I know it's been a long journey for you
Facing every right and wrong
It's okay to let your tears out
You've been holding them for too long

The days were never easy for you
And the nights didn't let you sleep
It's okay to apply a healer to your wounds
They are indeed deep

Yes every inch of your heart suffered
You are a hero without a cape
It's okay to shatter and rejoin your pieces
The puzzle definitely needs a new shape

Chunks in your throat
Anxiety attacks made you breathless
It's okay to cut off toxicity from your life
Calm down, you can clear this mess

Every ignorance was a lesson
You've been growing throughout
It's okay to shout when it feels heavy
In all these days your silence has been so loud

You've seen your swollen eyes
And witnessed every pain
Its okay to restart it is not a race
Take a deep breath and give yourself a chance again

Trust me you gave your best
Don't you dare to carry this guilt along
It's okay to break sometimes
In this whole life you've been acting strong.

SUBALAKSHMI

S. A. SUBALAKSHMI is a student at the Thiruvalluvar University currently taking up a Bachelor degree in English. As an English student she has trained to perform in writing and trying to improve her knowledge. She always loves to write her happiness and feelings in the wordings. She enjoys her day by day with happiness. She need best friends to share about her feelings and happiness in her life. She enjoyed every moment with happiness.

SISTER'S LOVE FOREVER

Some days she will hug you
Some days she will bug you
But you will always be.... sisters

Some days you will love her
Some days you will shove her
But you will always be..... Sisters

Some days you will laugh together
Some days you will cry together
But you will always be....sisters

At times you will wish, she would just go away.....
At times you will cry when, she must go her way....
But you will always be.... sisters
No matter what happens or what you go through

When you need understanding and a love that is true.....

Your sister's the one.....you   can always turn to.....

A SISTER LIKE YOU

Someone who will understand
Who knows the way I feel
In every situation
Her concern is very real....

Someone who has walked my ways
Who knows my every need
Times when she would see me cry
Her heart would nearly bleed...

Everyone should have a sister
Just the way I do
Richly blessed is what I am
To have a sister like you.....

KUMARA DHARMASEELAN

Kumara Dharmaseelan is just 23 who is pursuing his graduation in the field of commerce and residing in Chidambaram town within TamilNadu. He is a Sea lover. His life is Imagination in his heart. He loves traveling and reading books. He keeps on learning the lesson that life teaches him.

Instagram Handle: Dharmaseelan.k6

SEA LOVER

With the blue sea
Maybe Both magazines
Are with my magazine
Put Breathing is daily
Faces scratched...

Between two fingers
Search and drag
In the middle
Of the front...

To make my dark
Cheeks blush is your
Little magazine
Kiss enough...?

The word is too dry
Even the saliva on
The tongue was
Dry on time...!
An epic for my
Angel...!

MEMORIES OF SILENCE

The sea wave is restless
The beating is palpable
Beats for you my
Heart

Widespread
The sea you
Occasional showers
I

The child rolls the ball
Just like playing
With your memories
Playing!

VENESSA ALBUQUERQUE

Venessa Albuquerque is a Graduate in Science in Anaeshesia Technology from South Goa. She spends more words on Poetry, but does like writing Fiction, short stories and Blogs. She prefers the Ink and Paper more than the screen as she says 'It just comes naturally'. She wants to be recognized by her writings. Her Parents have supported her constantly and that's why we say Family is 'Constant'.

Instagram Handle: vba_2711

MESSAGE FROM YOU

As the wind blew
I used to ask it whether
There's a message from you

As the wind took
Not only my hair
But my heart and soul away

As the wind blew daily
I kept asking it the same
And it blew faster and harder

This went on and on
Until the wind in my life
Stopped speaking to me

I thought to myself
The blowing wind can't leave
Can't leave without answering me

It was then I knew
The blowing of the wind
And blowing harder on every question
Was itself a message from you.

UNTIL IT'S ALL GONE

I pretty well know this feeling
It's kind of weird kind of empty
Little bit of sorrow more of sadness
It's about regret and about going away
It's never yet over
Until it's all gone away

The inner me tells me all
The music used to be all
Little of the rhythm, more of the beats
Every minim and crochet, a tie
It has never felt so empty
Until it all went away

Crazy like hell, I went to tell
Not finding my music,
or music doesn't find me
just there's no coming back
and it felt all vanished
until it had all gone….

But the light at the end of the tunnel
The music I thought was running away
Was here holding up to me
For now there are no worries
As all the fears now I see
Until it's all gone

Flairs and Glairs, a platform by a student for the students. We are esteemed youth struggling to carve out our path for our future and we follow a basic mindset Since everyone is not born with all-round skills. Joining hands with people who are born to execute it with perfection is the best way to evolve. Self-Evolution is the need of the hour but, evolving as a community is what we strive for. The initiative as kickstarted by, Founder- Mr. Shubham Shah with the motive to utilize the skillset and talent of writing has now a team of 10+ people who are actively participating into newer forms of learning and discovering talents among youngsters. We Provide platform and services like Publishing opportunities, Open mics, Workshops, Hands-on training. Operating with Brand Name of Flairs and Glairs (Publication House), we offer the chance of elevating a passionate writer to an esteemed author With Brand name Teekhe Zasbaaat. We bring to you an opportunity to get accustomed with the Public Speaking and Presenting of Thoughts along with regular challenges to brush up your inking spirit. The newest initiative to extend our services we introduced in a new writing Platform- The Glittering Fables and Ink Over Tears.

We Choose to Fly Like A Falcon than to be

a Leg Pulling Crab.

To Know More: Infoline – 7781900870
Mail Us At-
flairsandglairs@gmail.com / info@flairsandglairs.in
Or Visit is at
www.flairsandglairs.com / www.flairsandglairs.in
Social Handles- @flairsandglairs @teekhezasbaaat